The Adventures
of
George and Mabel

Based on an Almost
(Kind of? Sort of? Could Be?)
True Story

Written by
Stefanie Hutcheson

I have tried to recreate events, locales, and conversations from my memories of them. In order to maintain their anonymity, in some instances, I have changed the names of individuals and places. I may have changed some identifying characteristics and some details such as physical properties, occupations, and places of residence.

This novella is dedicated to the ones I love.

A friend once told me how she got the idea for her novel. She explained there were these characters in her head, begging for her to tell their story. I didn't really relate to that well until. Until the challenge came up in my writing class for us to complete a work suitable for publication before the fall season of 2019.

I assumed I would just polish up and publish some of my *Wandering Through The Bible* Blogs. I didn't really consider myself much of a novelist. I have written several poems and short stories but didn't feel I had the patience to write a novel. Dialogue was something I hadn't experimented much with, and honestly? Taking the time to insert all of the punctuation marks that would be necessary--and especially all of those quotation marks!?--made me exhausted before I even began. Thus, I put aside that notion of me writing a book. Until.

Until one day on vacation, my husband Steve and I were headed towards Myrtle Beach. There was a box truck in front of us, driving a smidge erratically. I joked about it and said that it would make a good story, especially if it was transporting something--or someones--illegally. My quirky young friend Valerie had years ago begun calling Steve and me "George and Mabel." Well, two and two started adding up and before I knew it, the adventures of George and Mabel began.

Or did they?

As I continued writing stories about them, I realized I was actually recreating my life the way I wished it had been. I was going on adventures, being the successful one, having a wonderful family and fine friends, and...well? Well, I was writing about the life I wished I had had. I should have made some better choices. I should have been more careful to whom I placed my pearls before. I especially should have been a better Christian.

And now? Through the words and the lives of The Harrisons? Now I get to! And, if you are reading these words, you get to too. The old saying "If I only knew then what I know now" gets to be your new choice also. Perhaps these fun little stories will resonate with you as you travel with George and Mabel through time and times. Reflect on some of the childhood memories they share, the adult situations they face, and the love? Oh, the love they share!

I've never written a book before (unless you count the one I wrote for one of my sisters but never gave to her). So this dedication is a bit wordy but there are just so many to whom this book is devoted to. Many are mentioned by name in this novella so I think I will let them see how they impacted these stories. Others, like Steve--my very own personal George-- deserve a shout out. Without him I would have been unable to create--ha! As if!--to *model* my main character after. For you see, even though Mabel is fabricated in many parts, George is pretty much true blue. Like Steve. So, Lover: thank you.

Valerie, obviously, gets credit for the names of the two adventurers. Watching her grow into the lovely woman she is has been an experience book-worthy in itself.

My Foothills Writers Group also deserves credit. If the challenge hadn't been issued, I would still be muddling through my blogs and perhaps wasted a gift that God has allowed me to share through my writing.

Nikki, Lisa, and Gena have generously and sweetly mentored and edited me in the completion of this work. Thanks, ladies!

And then there are Rose, Linda, Jean Anne, Karen, Dedra, Beth, Donna, Virginia, Mary, Palma, Sara-- as well as the late Betty, Clella, and another Lisa-- who consistently have read my blogs and stories through the years. Their support warmed my heart on many occasions.

Anne Lamott once said: *"You own everything that happened to you. Tell your stories. If people wanted you to write warmly about them, they should have behaved better."* (Anne Lamott, *Bird by Bird: Some Instructions on Writing and Life,* 1995). Therefore, to those of you who did behave, this book is for you. And to you misbehavers? Hmn.

Lastly and most importantly, I would like to dedicate this book to my Lord and Saviour Jesus Christ. His longsuffering with me has had no bounds. Through His mercies, grace, and love my second chances have been many. Thank You, Father, for more opportunities to be better.

Table of Contents

Road Trippin'

"Hey George: what do you want to do today," Mabel asked.

"The same thing I want to do every day," he replied with a smile. Mabel waited for the oft-quoted "Take over the world" sentence that George often said in homage to one of his favorite cartoons, *Pinky and the Brain*. Instead, wisely, he said, "Whatever you want me to, Red."

"Let's go for a drive! I've been missing seeing the water. Shall we pick one of our cards or do you have a destination in mind?"

Months ago they had written on index cards their "Bucket List" of places they wanted to go to. Mabel kept them on hand for when they couldn't decide what to do on certain days--like this one.

"Why don't we head up Interstate 40 towards Lake Norman? We rarely drive that way. Besides, I've been craving some brisket. Maybe we can find us a nice barbeque spot for lunch. Sound good?"

He smiled as Mabel agreed and went off to get her things ready. That woman couldn't seem to go anywhere without her phone, a camera (yes, even though there was one on her device), her wallet, and a notebook. *Again*, George wondered, *wasn't that why "smartphones" were designed: to have all of these tools so one wouldn't have to pack a suitcase to go on a small venture?* He patiently waited for his love to finalize packing her suitcase--her purse, he meant.

Within minutes they were off. Mabel adjusted the iPod to play tunes from the '70s and '80s and was soon singing along to Alabama, John Denver, Foreigner, and Journey. George really liked Steve Perry's voice and found himself joining in to one of his favorite songs by them, "Faithfully." They smiled at each other and continued, appropriately, on their own journey.

Family had always been important to these two. Although they had no children of their own, they were quite fond of their extensive family, courtesy of George's two brothers and their wives (they had seven kids between them) and Mabel's sister Valerie (who had two of her own). It was rare that the Harrison Household didn't have monthly visitors who slept over as often as their parents would allow.

Mabel's thoughts turned toward Valerie, as the lyrics from "Solid" played. "Remember how ditzy Valerie is, bless her heart? She has the hardest time keeping things straight! Why, just last Tuesday when we were chatting on the phone, she says to me:

'Mabel, I was watching my stories the other day and that homewrecker Lucy was trying to tear apart her friend Felicia's marriage. She always wanted Frisco to herself. Does she not know her Bible?! Especially where it says what God has joined together, let no man pull us under?'

It was all I could do to not laugh out loud!"

George chuckled and recalled another incident when Valkyrie (his pet name for his sister-in-law) misquoted scripture. His brother's wife Jade had been preparing a fashion show for the girls at the local high school to share their used prom dresses. He'd proudly shown Val her Facebook post.

"Humpf" she had sniffed. "Looks like she needs to be catching up on her Bible instead, especially the part about studying to show herself a prude. Oh my cow, George! I'd never let my daughter leave the house in a dress like that, much less broadcast her wares all over Spacebook." She couldn't even call that media network by its correct name.

Suddenly Mabel exclaimed, "Watch out, George!"

The box truck ahead of them was veering sharply left and then right as it tried to adjust itself before completely going into the adjacent lane.

"Ugh! I wonder if he was on his cell phone. Dern texters! Or maybe he's sleepy?"

Mabel's mind and tongue often had quite a hard time keeping up with the other. George reached over and patted her on the leg, telling her it was okay, he was aware, when suddenly the truck lurched again.

"Oh my goodness! I sure hope he doesn't have breakable things in there. Crazy driver! Pass him as soon as you can, honey, and let's not be one of his casualties."

On a good day, Mabel was a nervous rider. She couldn't stand for a vehicle to be in front of her, blocking her view, nor could she tolerate being behind a diesel. The smell was too much for her delicate nostrils. Craning her neck to help, she watched for the opportunity for George to move in the other lane.

Unfortunately, it was a busy morning on the interstate. There didn't seem to be an opening and then, to make matters worse, the road was being repaved. Signs indicated that it would be down to one lane for the next two miles. Sighing, Mabel kept a close eye on the truck, hoping this new bump in the road would keep the driver ahead of them alert and safe. But, just in case it didn't, she reached for her handy dandy notebook and jotted down its license plate.

"George, get a little closer. I can't tell if it's from New York or New Jersey." Raising an eyebrow at Mabel's about-face concerning safe driving, George tried to inch a tad closer. Mabel was nearly perching on the dash, feverishly writing down digits.

"That's odd," she said. "I don't see any other kind of markings on that truck. No make or any bumper stickers. Don't they usually have at least one that says 'How's my driving? Call 1-800-blah blah blah' on them? But this truck..." she hesitated. "This truck doesn't have *anything* to distinguish it. Almost like it's on purpose, so that no one can identify it. George!"

He nearly jumped out of his seat. Was there a pothole he didn't see?

"Don't scream at me, Red. I'm right here. You know how I get when you..."

"George, hush a minute. Please, love. I just now remembered something I heard on the radio the other day. It was when I was researching us a place to stay at the beach. It was odd because I had just been on Google, reading about a recent surge in..."

"Mabel, can you please just get to the point? No offense, but you can tend to chase rabbits during our conversations."

Uh oh. Did I just say that out loud? George glanced her way and wondered. But thankfully Mabel was still chattering away, as though he'd not interrupted.

"...and they said there was a lot of human trafficking going on in Myrtle Beach. Can you believe it, George? *Human trafficking!* In our own neck of the woods! Oh, how that hurts my heart, love, and makes me worry about our babies."

Even though some of their nieces and nephews were in their teens, Mabel still referred to them as babies. She continued, "They say they grab them from places like the mall, or bowling alleys. You know, places where it *used* to be safe to let your kids have some freedom for a little while? Well, apparently *nowhere* is safe anymore."

The truck in front of them seemed to be under control now. It was actually even going slower than the posted speed limit, and George began to relax a little. He started to turn the volume back up to distract her but Mabel wasn't quite through.

"George! I just had a horrible thought!"

Waiting for her to continue, he patiently took a sip of his water. He offered her a swig but she shook her head.

"What if that truck in front of us is carrying a bunch of kids, George? Or drugs? Or some other sort of nefarious cargo?"

They had just passed a road sign with the Highway Patrol's number, asking motorists to report unsafe drivers or road conditions. This only egged Mabel on.

"Did you get that number, George? I think it was SHP38...but I didn't get the rest of it. Did you?"

George again shook his head and tried to change the subject.

"Let's talk about where we're going to eat. I'm getting hungry. Are you, sweetie? Besides, how often does something like this happen in real life, Red? I've been watching that truck now for the past few minutes and it seems fine. Maybe the driver just dropped her phone or spilled her coffee back there." George always assumed a female was behind the wheel whenever erratic driving took place.

Knowing he was probably right, Mabel decided to herself to let it go...unless. Unless the driver started acting kooky again or if she saw another Highway Patrol sign because then it would be...well, a sign. She reached for the volume knob, turned it up, and joined in with Stevie and Tom singing about not dragging each other's hearts around.

Almost relaxing, Mabel opened her window to let some fresh air in. They were back to the interstate being completely opened again and George began to inch his way into the other lane so they could pass the box truck and whatever cargo was inside of it. Casually glancing at it and trying to see a glimpse of the driver, Mabel felt more than saw the swerve of the vehicle as it once again seemed to lose its balance. Quickly it righted itself as Mabel met the eyes of the driver. It all happened so fast but she could almost feel his menacing gaze boring into her curious one. It made her shiver.

George was not unaware of this and reached over, once again patting her leg. "Red? It's okay, dear. Let's concentrate on the fun we're going to have. Why don't you start looking for an interesting sign for a place to eat? Besides, don't we have some better scenery to be looking for?"

He was right and Mabel googled "restaurants near me" trying to find a good place to satisfy that fierce noise going on inside of George's belly. Finding one that sounded interesting she kept her eyes peeled for Exit 113. They were ahead of the truck anyway and out of sight, out of mind. Right?

It was about then that she saw another billboard on the left side of the interstate, reminding drivers that all lives mattered. A moment later, she saw the one she'd been privately praying about, quickly jotted down the correct numbers this time, and made a deal with George.

"What if, just to be safe, I call this in? I just tell them the facts, that a driver is either sleepy or distracted, but nonetheless seems to not be in full control? I won't say my suspicions; I'll just let them take it from there. It probably is nothing, love, but...at least this way I'll know I did my part. Then we'll find you some brisket and me some sweet tea. This water is getting tepid!"

George agreed to her bargain, knowing there'd be no peace until he did and preferring to have his wife's full attention. After all, wasn't this why he retired: so they could spend more time together?
He checked the rearview to see if the truck was near. It was. He gave Mabel the thumbs-up sign and she pushed the last number. She reported the facts, was met with little interest by the operator who said she'd forward the information, asked what mile marker they were on, and which direction they were heading.

The call ended and soon Mabel was singing again, feeling she had done her good deed for the day. George joined in and together they butchered for the umpteenth time "Love in the First Degree" and left their cares behind them.

Not long after, they were seated in a booth at JD's Smokehouse in Rutherford College. Blissfully they were licking the sauce off of their fingers and completely unaware of a "Breaking News" story playing on a nearby tv. A routine traffic stop near Hickory had yielded an illegal load of young immigrants on their way to being sold on the black market. An anonymous tip from a driver on Interstate 40 had led the Highway Patrol to investigate this truck and at this time, the driver was not cooperating. The vehicle had stopped for diesel near Morganton and people nearby had heard a lot of loud and strange noises coming from it while the driver had gone inside to pay. A concerned citizen called 911. The local police became involved but by the time they arrived on the scene, the truck was already gone.

Meantime, according to the reporter, the driver was now being detained on the interstate because a Highway Patrolman noticed the box truck's tag was expired (a fact that had gone unnoticed by Mabel), and had pulled the vehicle over. As he was issuing the citation, Sergeant Helderman heard what he thought was the cry of a small child from the back of the truck. He immediately called for backup.

The driver was arrested soon after and the kids were being taken care of by local agencies. "As the Good Book states, all things do work together for good," was the soundbite used by a smiling social worker named Libby.

The breaking news ended with the excited reporter stating, "A heartfelt thank you is being said by many grateful parents as their missing children will soon be reunited with them. Whoever you are, unknown motorist, may God bless you for reporting this.

"Trust your gut, folks," the reporter ended earnestly, "for you just never know when someone needs you to be their hero."

While Mabel went to the bathroom, George paid their hostess Mary for the meal, declaring that this was the best brisket he'd ever eaten and that he and his wife would come back soon. As always, he asked for change for a dollar. Mabel came out of the restroom and smiled as she watched him insert the quarters into the gumball machines for some lucky kid to find. George, sensing her presence, turned to her with a sheepish grin and said, "Ready to go, Red?"

Taking his hand, she thought for the umpteenth time *Oh, how I love this man!*

Thursdays at the Harrisons

It was a typical Thursday evening at the Harrison household. Mabel was in her comfy brown recliner, playing online Binga (as little Amber called it--when she wasn't climbing all over the furniture, that is). George was puttering about, making sure he'd put up all of his screwdrivers so that he could spend the next couple of hours watching an old detective show he liked on the Nextflix (what one of the twins had dubbed the popular alternative to cable tv). Not many folks today can solve a crime like Lieutenant Columbo could.

All of a sudden, Mabel cried out. Startled, George jumped, nearly knocking his head into the opened toolbox. Thinking perhaps she'd had a spasm as she often was prone to do, thanks to her Restless Legs Syndrome, he courteously called out, "You okay, Red?"

Mabel was feverishly typing away at her keyboard while laughing in disbelief. Her fingers could not seem to keep up with her mind, not an uncommon thing if you knew Mabel.

"George, you aren't going to believe this!"

She kept on pecking while trying to talk. Her words were indistinguishable.

"What is it, dear?" As he placed the last flathead in the box, he patiently awaited her response.

She paused long enough to give him a look to let him know whatever had her this spellbound on the intranet (George's lingo for internet) was pretty exciting. In an exuberant tone, she breathed almost rapturously, "Geraldine!"

Her eyes had a dreamy, faraway look to them and he wondered which planet she was on now. He only knew of one Geraldine, a former friend and suite- mate of Mabel's from their college days.

"I always wondered what happened to her. And now, of all places, I have found her, George...in a Bingo room. Of all places!"

Mabel's fingers were still hammering away, making George wonder when those keys were finally going to cry out that they'd had enough.

"Didn't she..." George started to ask but he was instantly shushed. Mabel's eyes had that crazy glaze they sometimes got when too many boxes were open in that wonderfully ditzy mind of hers.

"I can't concentrate on you, her, and...and..."

Suddenly Mabel's tone changed.

"Oh no! *No*! I was just about to send her a friend request!"

Her fingers were oddly silent.

"What happened, Red? Did Jimmy Dean high hat you or something?"

"Jimmy Dean" was what George fondly called their old pal. Mabel always suspected it was because of Geraldine's penchant for those tiny little smoked sausages the cafeteria used to serve for breakfast way back in the day. Gerry seemed to never get enough of them. Or maybe it was because George liked to give certain folks "special" names that he felt somehow related what they meant to him, as well as helping him to better remember what to call them to let them know he, ahem, appreciated their presence in his and Mabel's lives.

Mabel just sat there, shaking her head, trying to figure out why--of all times!--the internet just had to go out when she was about to touch base with her long lost buddy. The memories were coming at her from all angles, reminding her of times of yore, times when she and Gerry would sit up long after they should have been asleep, talking and laughing about any and everything under the sun. An angry tear slid down her cheek as frustration set in.

George came over and rubbed her foot, trying to think about how best to help and not fix this. He'd already been in the dog house countless times for trying to fix things that Mabel insisted were not broken but instead that he only needed to hear her vent her frustrations about. And, it wasn't as if he could repair this, he told himself. Best to just give Red a few moments to simmer.

He hadn't given a second thought to Jimmy Dean in years. Surely her name hadn't even been spoken in a while. Best he could remember, she was off on a cruise ship or gallivanting around Spain. That must have been, what? In the late '90s? No, that couldn't be right. The change of the century nearly twenty years ago oft-made it hard to categorize the 2000-2010 era. What does one call that anyway: The Aughts?

Mabel sniffled and sadly closing the laptop.

"Oh, George! I couldn't believe my eyes when I saw that name pop up in the chat room. Honestly, you know, Geraldine is a fairly common name. I wasn't really even paying attention until she and another Bingo player were exchanging items. When I saw that her info was Geraldine Gerald Buchanan, from Pikeville, Tennessee, I knew there was no way this could be a coincidence! Gerry! *My* Gerry!"

She didn't continue but George could almost hear her rendition of what was supposed to be Frankie Valli and the Four Seasons' hit song "Sherry Baby" but with his wife's quirky sense of humor, she had changed the words to "Gerry, Gerry baby." He could almost picture them, dancing up the stairway, loudly singing without a care on their way to Ms. Verhulst's Writing Workshop Class while he hung back, trying to not let others know he was with them.

She heatedly went on. "I was just about to click on her profile picture to make sure when that danged ol' internet went kaputz!"

George thought if she could have gotten her leg up high enough she would have kicked that "danged ol' computer." He saw her reach for the mouse and wondered if she was thinking about throwing it at the cable modem or router across the room. Just in case, he moved a little to her left.

She was actually reaching for her phone and trying to connect to it via the wifi, but then angrily exhaling as she realized that it wouldn't allow the connection to her phone either. When he realized that meant there wouldn't be a good case for Columbo to solve tonight, George himself got a little disappointed.

Knowing Mabel as well as he did, he meandered to the back room, spent a few minutes rummaging about, and soon Mabel heard a satisfied grunt.

"Ta-da! Look what I found."

In his sweet hand was their college yearbook and Mabel just smiled. She knew what he was doing and her love for this man that has been at her side for going on three decades now just made her feel, well, kind of like a schoolgirl again.

Knowing it could be hours before Charter Spectrum got things back up and running, Mabel grinned and said, "I'll go make the popcorn."

She started to rise from the chair but first, she reached out her hand. Gallantly, George lifted it to his lips, placed a resounding smooch on it, and helped her up. With a twinkle in his eyes, he asked: "Uh, Red? Can you make pancakes and sausage instead? I think it might be a long night."

Mabel's Story

Hi. My name is Mabel. Mabel Lynn McKinney Harrison, to be more precise. I guess it's time we got to know each other a little bit better seeing as how you're reading all of these stories about me. Hang on! It might get crazy.

To begin with, I was born in a small town. Well, the real truth is, I wasn't actually *born* in a small town because it was too small to even have a hospital. A clinic was nearby but Lulu Mom would have none of that. Therefore, I was born in Asheville, North Carolina, and was raised in my hometown: Burnsville.

My birth date is December 9th, 1967. I am the oldest of two girls. My parents are Lula Mae Robinson McKinney and Jake (Big Jake to his friends) Dedrick McKinney. I have a younger sister, Valerie Virginia (sometimes called "VV" when I am feeling especially tender towards her), who was born in 1970.

My story is simple. I went to elementary school at Clearmont, spent the next three years at Cane River Middle, and then I was able to go to the town's only high school, Mountain Heritage. Go Cougars!

My days were spent on the farm where my family and I raised tobacco, gardened all different kinds of vegetables, and planted love. Yeah, it sounds corny, I know, but that's how it was.

After attending each summer during high school, I dreamt of being the director of the Upward Bound Program. I enrolled in Mars Hill College in Madison County, North Carolina. I loved that place, which is why George and I live here. I finished my education degree and George and I married in the summer of 1990.

I enjoyed being an assistant under Barbara for a few years. When she decided to pursue her love for teaching and resigned from UB, my dream of being the director came true! I stayed in that position for several more years until Mars Hill lost its funding for this wonderful organization and discontinued it.

I consider myself to be a simple and fairly uncomplicated woman. It doesn't take much to please me. I've never been a girly girl so getting my hair done, my nails manicured, and weekly facials have never been on my agenda. I sometimes still chew my fingernails--if the truth be told--and my face? Kind of a cross between Emma Stone and Kate Winslet. Momma always said "pretty is as pretty does." Therefore, I have tried to keep a pleasant look on my face, in my heart, and in my actions. I feel like I did well. I hope I did well.

George and I didn't have kids of our own. We really wanted to. Hoped to. But somehow it just didn't seem to be part of the plan.

Between our families, we have a grand total of nine nieces and nephews. We spoil them royally! They enjoy coming to our house, spending the night, and on occasion, the weekend with us. All of us try to get together at least monthly. Each year all of the Harrison and Revis clans meet for family gatherings and/or reunions. We like to celebrate each and everyone's birthdays, anniversaries, graduations, and achievements. We just like to be together. Plus, we really like cake!

My sister Valerie and I have almost always been close, even though there were times she really tried me. Although we shared many of the same friends during our high school years, she always looked up to me the most, even though I wasn't very tall (unlike Big Jake).

VV can be a little bit ditzy. Some would say it's because she got whacked on the head one time too many during some of our more exuberant play times. For instance, there was this time when she and I were wrestling on my four-poster bed. We got a little rough and before I knew it she went over the side, hitting her sweet little head on a nearby hope chest that happened to have a sharp edge.

There was some blood. Lots of tears. Momma and Daddy came rushing in, wondering what I had done to make Valerie scream in such "agony." Scooping her up in their arms, we rushed to the hospital in Asheville, where Valerie received eight stitches--and lots of attention.

She was the belle of the ball and milked it for all it was worth. Maybe that explains part of why she has memory issues now. Maybe not. She is the blonde one of the family. Me? I am the one with red hair--and sometimes a temper. Pale-faced, freckle-faced, sunburn-prone, slightly pudgy, and very inquisitive. These would be better words to describe me: as a child, and to some degree, as a 50-plus-year-old woman.

Daddy passed away a few years ago. George and I had settled in Mars Hill while Valerie and her hubby Will lived in Weaverville, a neighboring town, with their two daughters, Amanda and Miranda. His loss was tremendous and his impact, like his name, was big.

Lulu Mom didn't want to live on the farm on Jack's Creek all by herself and neither Val nor I had an interest in continuing that legacy. Therefore, Mom is now settled nicely in a local retirement home--the kind where the seniors go on day trips, out to eat, take an occasional cruise, and play bingo. Lots of bingo. I like to go play with them some on Monday nights because that is one of my favorite games. Plus it gives George a break. We can't spend every waking moment together now, can we?

Mom is in her late seventies now. VV and I take turns visiting with her and often we go together to see her, to take her to lunch, or to go get her hair fixed. When she can fit us in, that is. She likes to go!

Her mind is starting to falter somewhat and the doctors told us she has the early symptoms of dementia. Right now, most of the time, she's okay. But it won't be long until we have to change her room at the retirement center into one of those where more assisted care is provided. Until then though, we are going to cherish every moment we have with this lovely lady, this woman we love so very much. Lulu Mom.

Well, I didn't mean for this to be so long. I only wanted to give you a snapshot of what my life has been like up until now. I was one of the fortunate ones who planned my timetable and knew that I wanted to retire early enough to be able to travel while I still had my health. While not rich, I am comfortable.

George is too. He retired after nearly 28 years with City Electric Supply Company. Now we spend our days and nights getting reacquainted and going on day trips around our lovely state of North Carolina, visiting with family, and devoting more time to our hobbies. I've started a blog and attend a weekly writing class. George stays busy with little projects here and there. Plus, he often teaches Sunday School. He's such a good teacher! And, did I mention the babies? How we love those kids!

How Deep Is Your Love. That might be the title for the chapter of the book that tells you how George and I first met. It was one of those encounters that happens once in a lifetime yet...it was one of those encounters that, when looked back upon, makes you realize that God does indeed work all things together for good.

Never Gonna Give You Up

As George went to the local range to hone up on his mediocre shooting skills, Mabel decided it would be a good time to catch up with her sister. She reached for her phone and dialed.

"Hel-looo Maybelline! I was just thinking about you." Mabel smiled, thinking to herself she'd caught Val at a good time.

"Hello yourself, Val-er-ie," Mabel responded, in a singsong fashion. The girls had grown up listening to pop music and rare was the occasion when a portion of some song lyric didn't make it into their conversations.

They exchanged pleasantries, got caught up on Val's daughters, and then discussed what to do with Lulu Mom for Mother's Day. Since Dad had passed, Momma was trying her best to stay independent. However, her girls kept a close watch on her and checked in with her often to make sure her needs were being met.

"I'd like to take her to my church this time, Mabes. If that's okay? We got a new choir director, Mike, and he's just so...so...oh, I don't know how to describe him."

Valerie broke off, and Mabel could picture her there, one hand on her hip and the other raised in the air, as though searching for just the right word.

"He takes certain scriptures and turns them into songs to help us to better memorize and apply them. It works! Like, do you remember that one from Jeremiah 29:11, Mabes? It goes like this:

> For I know the plans I have for
> you," declares the LORD, "plans
> to prosper you and not to harm
> you, plans to give you hope and
> a future.

That one, Mabes?"

Val took a breath and Mabel was pleased that for once her sometimes ditzy sister actually quoted the verse correctly. Mabel smiled to herself and started to respond but she was too slow.

"Well, Pastor Mike--I guess you'd call him a pastor? 'Minister of Music Mike' doesn't quite sound right, does it?"

Valerie was known to chase a rabbit or two.

"Anyways, Pastor Mike and his wife Becky--she plays the piano so beautifully, Mabes. I could listen to them all day. In fact, last Sunday, she and Mike and that sweet daughter of theirs, Alechia, sang that song we used to sing as kids, 'Almost Home,' that just made me ready to turn my ticket in and board the next train to heaven!"

Glancing at her watch and seeing the seconds turn into minutes, Mabel gently interrupted her chatty sister, knowing if she just let her keep yakking, she'd never have George's lunch ready by the time he got home.

"Umm, Val? You were saying you'd like for us to go to church with you and take Mom there. Right?"

"Wellll, *actually* I was talking about Minister Mike," she huffed at her. "If you'd let me finish, please!"

Mabel could picture Val's right foot angrily tapping away as her indignation over being interrupted was reflected in her sister's voice. But, never one to hold a grudge for long, she was soon back in Val Land, continuing as if she'd never stopped talking.

"Minister Mike told us how--and you're gonna love this, Sis--how so many secular songs will point us to Jesus if we just look for Him in them. He went on to sing a song and as that sweet Becky was playing along, I found myself back in time, Mabes! You'll never believe what song he used for this verse!"

Dramatic pause. "I'll give you a hint."

Mabel waited patiently, putting the bacon in the oven to crisp up just the way George liked it.

"They weren't strangers to love."

Silence.

"Nothing, Mabes? Okay. Here's hint number two. They knew the rules."

Mabel began slicing a tomato. "And?"

The words were slightly familiar but she couldn't resist teasing Val.

VV nearly exploded. Again Mabel could picture that right foot tapping away. She went on.

"I've got to make you understand!"

Excitedly, Mabes joined in. *"Never gonna give you up!"*

"Yes!" Valerie happily exclaimed.

By now, both sisters were singing merrily to this ditty by Rick Astley. They broke off, giggling, and just enjoyed the moment.

It was about then that Mabel heard George pull up. Bringing the gabfest to a quick close, she arranged the time and such with Valerie to meet at church, who closed the prattle with a few last words.

"Mabes? I just love you! I can't wait to see you and George and Lulu Mom tomorrow. Be a dear and make sure her shoes match this time, okay? Remember what happened at Easter?"

Mabel indeed remembered, reflecting on the absurdity of one blue loafer paired with a lime green sandal on Mom's feet. They did, *technically,* match her outfit but probably would have looked better had both shoes matched each other rather than the stripes in Mom's sweater.

As she pushed the bread down in the toaster, Mabel said her goodbyes, reached in the 'fridge for the Swiss cheese and mayonnaise, and heard George enter through the garage. As he walked in, he could hear his beloved humming a familiar tune.

Slipping up beside her and reaching for a hot slice of bacon, George joined in. He sang about how he was never going to give up bacon and Mabel laughed.

Playfully she swatted his hand from reaching for another piece, and declared, "George Jones Harrison, I know the plans I have for you. Plans to not harm you--but *only* if you save some of those slices for me!"

Puzzled, George stared at her, and asked, "Have you been talking to your sister again?"

The Summer of '78

It was the summer of 1978, the summer of Abba, "Grease," The Commodores, and the debut of The Bee Gees' little brother Andy. The movie tunes from "Saturday Night Fever" were still rocking their ways to the American Top 40.

Big Jake had often gone to Sliding Rock when he was growing up. He wanted his girls to be able to make some memories of their own there. So, when school let out for the summer, Mabel and her family, along with two of Mabel's best friends--Brenda and Lisa Jo--spent a weekend in Brevard, North Carolina.

As the radio played pop hits, the girls--except for Val--sat in the back seat of the Ford station wagon, giggling and singing, and whispering. Valerie was not a happy camper. She hated being the odd woman out, even if she was only eight-years-old. Fuming, she plotted her revenge. Oh sure: next year would be "her turn" and she'd get to invite two of her friends but next year might as well be a lifetime from now.

As Brenda sang John Travolta's part and Lisa Jo channeled her inner Olivia Newton-John, Mabel alternated between which part to sing along to, but mostly just joined in the chorus. If Valerie had to hear them singing about being the one that each other wanted one more time, she thought she might just scream, *honey,* even though her foot somehow couldn't keep still and her arms tapped along her legs in tune with the song.

After they had checked into The Sunset Motel, the girls changed into their swimsuits and were ready for the drive to Sliding Rock. Valerie had recently learned how to swim and was quite excited to show off her skills because--even though she was the older one--Mabel was still a big chicken in the water. Valerie hoped she got to show up her big sister and get to have some of the attention put on her this weekend.

From the bathroom, Lisa Jo was oh so dramatically singing into her hairbrush about there not being anywhere to hide and being devoted to some unknown kid. Probably that boy Jerry who rode her and Mabel's bus, if Valerie's snooping into her sister's diary was any indication.

I'll say you're out of your head, Lisa Jo, thought Valerie. Rushing to the car, she climbed in the back seat, only to be shooed away as Mabel and Brenda got in from the other side and Mabes laughingly said "The word is grease, squirt. Slide on up front, little sister!"

Valerie continued plotting her revenge.

At the same time, another family was also visiting this tourist attraction. George, Mark, and Jim Harrison were making trains and going down this waterslide provided by Mother Nature as their parents looked on from the overlook. Grady and Daisy tried to allow the boys freedom to grow up without too much hovering and they knew they could count on George to be diligent with their younger sons.

Sliding Rock was a busy placc. At this period of time, there were no lifeguards on duty because this recreational site hadn't been "discovered' by too many folks other than the locals and past visitors.

George was like a fish in the water and loved this swimming hole with its cool water waiting for him to bask in when he reached the bottom of the rock. Mostly a loner because of the age difference between his brothers and him, George always felt responsible for them and while he reveled in the brisk water rushing all about him, he still felt like he had to be on guard all of the time. He kept a watchful eye at all times, trying to make sure his "boys" stayed safe--and that they weren't being a nuisance.

When they finally had had enough, he monitored their every move until they reached the safety of their parents waiting at the ropes. George breathed a sigh of relief as he took another dunk in the pool before starting to make his own trek back up the hill.

It was about this time that Valerie decided she was tired of being the baby. While Mabes, Brenda, and Lisa Jo prissed about in their bathing suits and worried about how they would be going into the water and not getting their hair wet, Val was ready to jump in. However, Mom and Dad insisted that even though yes, she was an excellent swimmer, no, she could not lead the chain of the four girls and would go down with them instead.

Seeing that they were still preoccupied with keeping their lips glossed and their ponytails primped, Val eagerly went down the rock, over and over, until finally her exhausted parents told her they needed a break and suggested she stand on the bridge and take some pictures since the girls finally seemed ready to take the plunge. Feeling honored to get to use the new Polaroid Camera that Daddy had recently purchased, Valerie agreed. Knowing she'd only have eight shots, she planned them wisely.

Mabel was still skittish about the water so once the decision had been made to slide, she wanted to be the last in line. Screeching the lyrics to "We Go Together," Brenda took the lead, with Lisa Jo in the middle, and Mabel holding on for dear life. The trio pushed their way to the spot where the water would take over and carry them to the bottom. How Mabel went from joyously laughing as the threesome began their descent to somehow losing her grip on Lisa Jo's waist is hard to figure out. As she neared the end of the excursion, she was somehow turned sideways. She felt the water rush over her and panicked. While Mabel went down down down, she didn't have time to think, to feel, to remember all of the lessons about holding her breath. Instead, she screamed--or tried to--and felt the water envelop her. In actuality, it only was a few seconds but to Mabel, it was a lifetime.

As her ponytail became loose, her red curls swirled about her, blocking her vision. Suddenly she felt two strong arms lifting her up as she violently kicked, forgetting again to relax, and her blue eyes blazed in fury until she realized she was being saved. As she surfaced and gasped for air, she felt the hands release her and lead her to the rope that would allow her to climb back to the top of the rock.

Her auburn tresses were now a mess and her pink ponytail ribbon was gone. As she turned to thank the one who had rescued her, Brenda came and tugged her arms and said, "Let's go. Stop being a spaz. To the bathroom. Now. My hair is a wreck!"

She and Lisa Jo were oblivious to Mabel's near-death experience. They were too busy trying to still look cool and not quite pulling it off. As they hurried to the restrooms, Mabel looked once more for her hero.

There he was! Standing next to the building that led to the changing rooms, there stood this tall, skinny kid. He'd been patiently tying his little brother's shoe. He barely looked up but when he saw those strawberry-blonde curls, he became mesmerized.

As though in a trance, he walked over to Mabel.

Words wouldn't come for either of them but it was as if something...electric seemed to pass through them. On an impulse she never could quite explain, Mabel reached over and kissed him. On the lips! Something she had never done before she was suddenly an expert at.

Though it lasted a mere second or two, its effect on George branded him for life. And, just as the playful waters of the Davidson River had pulled these two into its current, George somehow knew that his life would never be the same.

"Ooh. Gross!"

"I'm telling Mom. George is kissing a *girl*!"

And from the bathroom exit, of course, there stood Brenda--once again mimicking John Travolta while Lisa Jo crooned about summer love happening so fast. They laughed at Mabel's first kiss and cackled over her meeting a cute boy. Completely mortified, Mabel ran into the bathroom, determined to put this hapless incident out of her mind--or at least try to.

But nobody laughed nearly as hard as Valerie. Held in her hand, for future ammunition, was the perfect shot of this historical moment of time. Tucking it into her backpack, she innocently joined the girls to tell them it was time to go. Smiling secretly to herself, she thought *I've got you now, Mabes!*

Big Jake

"Hey Red. What's for supper tonight?"

George was making his plans for the day and wanted to know if he should eat a large lunch out or save his appetite for some of Mabel's delicious cooking. Say what you want to about Mabel's mom Lulu and her fading mind: that lady sure did teach Mabes how to cook when it mattered!

Mabel had been pondering that very thing, seeing as how nothing pleased her more than being in the kitchen, cooking up a feast for her man. For real! As a child, she was often found at her mother's elbows, following her every move, and stirring as many pots as were allowed. She was always short so a stool was often perched near the stove for those moments when Mom "needed" some help--or a fudge pan sopped.

"How about a tasty roast beef, some deviled eggs, rice, gravy, and maybe some of Aunt Alice's green beans? I think we have a jar or two left from last summer's harvest."

George's belly responded in anticipation. Bellowing a loud, hungry growl, he started to back himself into the kitchen.

"My goodness woman: I now remember why it is I married you! Besides those beautiful blue peepers, I mean." He winked at her as he continued his rave.

"Mmn-mmn! That sure does sound wonderful, Red! Just how long anyway does it take a roast beast to cook? Maybe I'll just stay home and we'll eat it for lunch?" He grinned, pulled her into his arms, and leaned down for a kiss.

Laughingly, Mabel pushed George away, giving him a gentle pat on his backside with the wood spoon that was in her hand. "Oh no, you don't, mister. Mark is counting on you to teach the twins how to site in the scopes for the bb rifles that you insisted they were old enough to have. Besides," she continued, "a roast takes a couple of hours to cook and believe it or not, dear" (this may have been said a touch emphatically) "I *do* have a life outside of this kitchen!"

They both laughed and enjoyed another sweet smooch before Mabel once again gave him the gentle push he needed to leave. Retirement was agreeing with them and even though it had just been the two of them for most of their married lives, they still couldn't seem to get enough of each other. *Life really is grand when one marries her best friend*, she thought to herself.

Sliding the roast beef into the oven, Mabel did a quick inventory to make sure she had all of the necessary ingredients for the rest of the planned meal. Kraft Mayo, Mount Olive Dill Pickles, and Grey Poupon for the eggs? Of course. Minute Rice? Check. She started to close the door when she noticed the red box of Duncan Hines German Chocolate Cake Mix next to the Folgers. Thinking how good it would be later with some coffee, she reached for it and as she did, noticed the calendar hanging on the fridge.

June 8.

Dad's birthday.

Coincidence? Hardly. Mabel didn't believe in those.

With a happy but melancholy sigh, she read the ingredients. As though she didn't know them by heart. Three eggs; a cup and a quarter of water; half a cup of oil. Add cake mix. Beat for two minutes. Pour into prepared pan. Bake for such and such amount of minutes at 350°.

Oh, Daddy! I miss you so!

Mabel recalled how every year he would ask her and Valerie to make him a special birthday dinner. "If you two girls are gonna be good wives like your pretty momma is, you gotta learn early how to cook, clean, and be cute. And there ain't much cuter than a woman in the kitchen, cleaning as she goes. Ain't that right, Lulu?"

Then he'd run, as his three "cuties" attacked. He'd turn on them suddenly, laughing and somehow managing to catch all three and smother them with kisses and tickles. After, while the womenfolk went back to their "duties," Big Jake (his childhood nickname because he was so tall) would go into the study and get out the Barry Manilow record albums. Soon he'd be crooning "Mandy" while Mabel, Mom, and Valerie tried not to laugh. Valerie declared early in life that this was her and Daddy's song and loved it so much that she named her firstborn child Amanda.

Sliding the roast beef over to make room for the cake in the oven, she continued to reflect on Dad and his love for Barry Manilow songs. She recollected the times she went away for the summer. The Upward Bound Program at Mars Hill College was her opportunity to learn more about what college would be like. Neither of her parents had been able to attend and wanted the best for their girls. So, for six weeks each summer before her sophomore, junior, and senior years of high school, Mabel would spend that portion of her summer with kids from neighboring counties, learning about all kinds of things, playing sports, and competing in activities against Western

Carolina University in Waynesville, who also sponsored an Upward Bound Program in their area of the state. Mars Hill was also where she had met Tammy, one of her best friends--still to this day.

Big Jake missed her dreadfully while she was gone. He'd make her mix-tapes (with the help of Val) and she'd listen to Hall and Oates, Air Supply, and The Eagles on nights when she felt lonely. But there were so many other things in her life then to focus on. She and Dad had a few arguments and her pubescent years were not ones she was always proudest of. She grew away from him and now--as she remembered how no matter how rotten she treated him, he had always welcomed her home with open arms--she let the tears fall. *Why was I such a prodigal daughter?*

Her daddy had been her hero. He was the one who taught her how to dance, to catch pop flies, to sow seeds that would turn into their sustenance later in the fall and winter. He taught her how to fish, to roller skate, and mostly, he taught her about the Lord.

"Mabel Lynn McKinney, no matter how far you go, you cannot outrun God's love. Nor mine. He gave His life for you and I would give you mine if I could. But I cannot, my darling daughter. But, Mabel Lynn, what I can give you," he'd said, reaching into his pocket, "is this New Testament. I've marked my favorite verses and carried this book with me ever since I received it back in 1963. Now I want you to have it."

She still remembered the verse inscribed on the first page from Romans 8:28, Daddy's favorite book of the Bible. It was:

> *And we know that all things work*
> *together for good to them that love*
> *God, to them who are the called*
> *according to His purpose.*

Big Jake died a few years back. That tobacco he grew for their livelihood cost him his. She missed him horribly, and as she placed the cake to bake in the oven, she thought she'd call Mom and see how she was handling today. She reached for the phone and dialed but didn't get an answer. *Just as well,* thought Mabel. *She might not even remember Dad, much less that this would be his birthday. No sense in causing her more confusion.*

Suddenly, from the living room, the words "I don't want to walk without you, baby" floated to the kitchen sink. Mabel was comforting herself with one last spoonful of the warm coconut icing she had just prepared and nearly jumped off her stool.

"George Jones Harrison! You almost gave me a heart attack!"

George stood in the hallway, right hand extended as he prepared to ask Mabel for this dance. With his other, he smiled sheepishly and reached behind him, and pulled out a large bouquet of sunflowers, Mabel's favorite.

Melting into fresh tears, Mabel rushed over to him. "Wha--"

Placing his fingers over her quivering lips, he replied, "Shh, my love. Don't talk. Just dance."

She allowed herself to be swept into his arms. The sweetness lasted about a minute when suddenly the music changed. A more upbeat tempo began as two little boys suddenly appeared from behind the couch, dressed in boas and high heels. They could barely stand up. From the living room closet appeared Mark and Melissa and they were singing into a karaoke microphone about a showgirl named Lola. Harry and Lloyd, giggling gleefully, grabbed big brother Shaun's arm and made him dance in a circle with them.

George suddenly tossed the sunflowers to the couch and started to tango with Mabel, while Mark, Melissa, and the boys began a line dance. Soon they were all collapsing in laughter. That is, until the smoke detector started blaring furiously.

"The cake!" Mabel shrieked and ran for the kitchen.

Thankfully, it was salvageable, as there had been something else that had spilled in the oven earlier that was causing the smoke alarm to shrill. George wasn't far behind, checking to see if the roast beef was okay--or rather, if his help was needed. Mmn-hmn.

George joked, "Whew! That was a close one, Red. I thought the roast beast might be through and we'd need a miracle!"

"Oh, George! You silly goose!" Mabel laughed, as she set the cake onto a cooling mat. "What am I going to do with you?"

"Hmn," George pondered, as he gave the icing bowl a quick swipe with his finger, placed it in his mouth, and smiled with satisfaction. "How about a weekend in New England?"

The Little Red-Haired Girl

George was in love. Total infatuation. While other kids his age were all about sports, George was all about the Little Red-Haired Girl. Early on Sunday mornings, he'd race down the stairs and go outside to fetch the *Hendersonville Times-News*. He'd rush to the dining room table, feverishly take all of the sections apart, and then place them carefully back together on the table because--even through his excitement to see if she was there--he was still a neat guy.

Finding the comics, George would take them to the living room, sprawl out on the floor, and excitedly find the *Peanuts* strip. He'd gloriously read each cartoon block, hoping against hope that *she'd* be there this week. The Little Red-Haired Girl. For some reason, after the summer's trek to Sliding Rock, George became enamored with this elusive love of Charlie Brown's. While he had always been a fan of Snoopy, that secret kiss that somehow his brothers didn't share after all with their parents had stirred something within his heart that Lucy, Sally, Eudora, Marcie, Peppermint Patty, and even that Frieda--with her naturally curly hair--had not.

He tried to keep it a secret. Being almost eleven-years-old was confusing enough. Some of his friends, like Junior and Michael, still played GI Joe after school while others were all about sports and trying to look and act cool for the upper middle-schoolers. Guys like Drake and Shep suddenly began wearing cologne and wearing their collars turned up. He wasn't sure what was up with that, pardon the pun, but he kept his lying normally.

George was a pretty good athlete and could hold his own with those seventh and eighth-graders so this didn't matter much to him and he thought he smelled okay without that extra Old Spice or Brut. Although he didn't deal with much pre-teen angst, just in case, he hid his fondness for this girl and pretended on those times he was "caught" seeking her out that he was doing so to entertain his kid brothers.

In October of 1978, his efforts paid off! There was going to be a primetime edition of *Peanuts*, called *It's Your First Kiss, Charlie Brown*. Being as there weren't that many television channels to choose from, George was able to convince the folks and brothers into watching it. And, sure enough, she was there! *Finally*. Even though that Lucy caused him to miss the field goal that would have won the game, somehow Charlie Brown still wound up being the hero because--for one night anyway--he got the girl.

Through the years, George continued following Charlie's story and became quite the *Peanuts* buff. He collected each Sunday's contributions to the comic strip (they were in color) and through the week, he'd valiantly try to clip each day's black-and-white portion of them.

He saved them all in scrapbooks and allowed only a couple of his closest friends to enjoy them with him. Mom and Dad never ran out of gift ideas for him and by the time he graduated from high school, he had quite the collection of *Peanuts* memorabilia items.

But when George entered Mars Hill College as a freshman, there just wasn't room in his small dorm room shared with his roommate Eric to display them. Thus, they stayed back in his place at home, awaiting his weekend visits, which became fewer and further between.

Few of his new friends knew about his enthusiasm for Charlie Brown--not that he was in any way or form ashamed of it! Rather, he just continued randomly collecting keepsakes from this portion of his childhood, not knowing how the subliminal message of Charlie Brown's love for the imaginary Little Red-Haired Girl was affecting his present life. Oh sure, for some reason (ahem) he'd found himself more attracted to red-headed ladies than the blondes and brunettes in his aurora (as Aunt Alice called "aura"). But it wasn't until he met and befriended Mabel Lynn McKinney during his sophomore year of school that it started to make sense. While George had not been obsessed with them, his passion did indeed lead him to be more drawn to these gingers than other lovely gals his age. It was as though, subconsciously, his dream girl just *had* to have auburn tresses. It would be another twenty-five years though before the final missing puzzle piece was in place and he would fully comprehend.

That's Her

One night during his sophomore year at Mars Hill, George and his roommate Walter were attending the final basketball game. While George was engrossed in the action on the court, Walter wasn't really the sports buff. He had come to college for one purpose and one purpose only: he wanted a wife!

During a timeout, George overheard him talking to someone--maybe one of his fellow Upward Bound counselors--about Sliding Rock. Piqued by the reference, George turned his head away from the ball game and instantly stared into the most alluring blue eyes he'd seen in years. As Walter and this beautiful creature continued chatting, George found himself mesmerized by this strawberry blonde and couldn't wait to get back to the dorm and question Walter about her. At the same time though, he felt he could sit on that hard, wooden bleacher forever and just listen to her sweet Southern dulcet tones.

He wasn't the only one who wanted to talk to Walter in private. Something about this friend of his who was trying not to eavesdrop on their conversation attracted Mabel like none other ever had. She didn't even know his name but, by grabs, she was most definitely going to find out! She kept glancing over Walter's shoulder and he half-heartedly murmured a quick introduction. They smiled at one another and started to say "hi" but the game was in its final seconds and the crowd kept getting in the way. The Lady Lions won and the crowd went crazy! Fans poured out onto the court. Celebrations began and she and her friends were jostled about. Walter and his handsome buddy were nowhere to be seen.

From that night on, though, it seemed like they were constantly running into each other. Although they had both been at Mars Hill for over a year, somehow their eyes had never met. Now? Their eyes were constantly seeking the others' out.

There was George, leaving Mrs. Hughes' English class just as Mabel was entering Dr. Sawyer's Old Testament class across the hall. How had she not ever noticed him before? He certainly was easy on the eyes. Later, in the cafeteria, George saw Mabel at the salad bar and suddenly decided pork chops were not what he really wanted for supper after all. He made his way over, used a funky French voice, and said, "Pardon me, Miss. Do you have any Grey Poupon?"

Mabel looked up, laughed, and replied, "But of course!"

They continued making their salads and found themselves heading towards the same table. Eric noticed George and called out, "Yo! Harrison! Over here."

Meanwhile, Mabel's friends Wendy and Karen were getting her attention and making room for her at the opposite end. Shrugging a bit sadly at each other, they joined their cronies.

Throughout the meal, their eyes wandered down the table and continued to search for the other's. They'd shyly smile at one another but were not able to talk any more that night. George had a study session planned with some guys from his Biology class. His buddy Tony needed to greatly impress Dr. McCloud with his insights and make up for some poor grades. George had offered to study with him to help him out, joking with him that his football prowess on the football field would only take him so far. Maybe some fancy footwork around the botanical grounds instead of Stephanie's dorm room might be more useful, George suggested.

The next day as she was coming back from a weekly tutoring session at Mountain Heritage, Mabel saw a slightly familiar soul on the road into town. He was so tall! As her car drew near, she realized it was George. He had been at the local daycare and was walking back toward campus.

Rolling down her window as she slowed the car, she called out, "Pardon me, sir. Would you happen to have any Grey Poupon?"

Delighted at this unexpected turn of events--not to mention that no one else was around this time to interrupt or distract--George put on a woebegone face, shook his head, and then brightened when he responded, "No, I haven't any. But I know a place where we can get some. If you'd be so kind as to give me a ride, I'll most gladly fetch you some. My lady," he added, with a twinkle in his blue eyes and, *was that a wink,* Mabel wondered?

Laughing, Mabel told him to get in and that she'd be happy to give him a lift.

"I'm quite heavy," George deadpanned. "Are you sure I won't hurt you?"

Their eyes met and without any hesitation at all, Mabel declared "Positive."

It was only a moment, only an nth of a second, but something profound seemed to pass between them. It was as though a seed took root in her heart and burst forth through her soul.

A horn honked from behind them and the spell was broken. George climbed in, buckled up, and yes: there it was again. He really *did* wink while saying something about how one can never be too careful when there were so many women drivers on the road these days.

Reaching for the radio dial to drown out his smarmy remark, Mabel sang along to "Hands to Heaven" emphasizing the word "pray" and giving George a sideways look while giving Old Elmer (her beloved Plymouth yellow station wagon) some gas before the now irate driver behind them honked again. It was pointless though. *He* drove on by, hollering something about it being a road, not a blessed pick-up stand. They looked at each other, broke into laughter, and started to drive down Main Street.

"Oh, Mabel? Speaking--or should I say 'singing'--of heaven, would you be interested in going to the FCA meeting with me on Tuesday?"

"Ha! I was planning on going there too. I try to not miss them," she responded. "I'd be honored to be your da--guest."

Embarrassed at what she had almost blurted out, she reached for the radio dial once more. Steve Winwood was singing "Valerie" and Mabel began telling George how she had a sister named Valerie. He told her of his brothers, Mark and Jim. Their conversation never lagged. For the next few hours, they talked about any and everything.

As they drove around Highway 70 towards Spring Creek, Mabel asked George, "So, what were you doing at the daycare, George? Making some new friends?"

George chuckled and explained. "Do you remember the PDS class we had to take? I was in Dr. Plaut's, the sociology teacher, and we had to choose a social project to do. Mine was to go and play with the little kids at the local daycare."

Mabel laughed. "Didn't we take that class as freshmen, George? What's the matter: did you not pass?" She hesitated. "You didn't fail, did you?" She thought he seemed relatively intelligent but maybe he wasn't.

Humbly, George kind of shook his head and said, "No: no I passed. I just didn't quit going."

Nothing more. Just those simple words.

Smiling inside, Mabel said to herself *So... he likes kids. Good to know.*

As they continued to talk and learn about each other, telling what they were there at school for, which dorm they lived in, what they wanted to do with their majors, and small details about their families, the trip to find some mustard became a distant memory. They drove all around Madison County while Mabel explained that she had loved this area since her high school days of being in

Upward Bound. Her dream, she told George longingly, was that one day she would live here.

It was about that time that George's stomach began rumbling, loudly, and they realized they had lost all track of time. The sun had set an hour ago. They had missed their chance to eat in the dining hall. Giving George a serious look, telling him she feared he might pass out from starvation, Mabel asked him if he'd like to go grab a hot dog at the Bantam Chef. George replied, once again with that cute wink of his, "Only if they have some Grey Poupon."

~~~~~~~~~~~~~~~~~~~~

Tuesday came and Mabel and George were going to the monthly gathering held in the Student Union for the FCA. They'd only been there a few minutes before George, politely excusing himself, left Mabel at her seat. Not sure what was going on, she turned self-consciously to her friend Jennifer and asked her what tonight's conference was to be about anyway? Jen told her that it was about dating and smirked at Mabel and said, "You know: kind of like what you and George are doing."

Mabel wasn't sure how to respond to that because, although she would love more than anything else to be seriously dating George, she just wasn't sure that they were there yet. It'd only been a couple of weeks since they met. Her wandering thoughts were interrupted when the guest speaker was introduced. Imagine her surprise when the name "George Jones Harrison" was called out. As he calmly approached the lectern, the students politely clapped and then listened for the next few moments as George gave his testimony.

He had a calm, easy-going manner. He spoke of how all through high school and college he had refrained from most of the dating scene. George revealed that he had encountered many lovely young women and had actually even gone to prom with a couple of them--but not at the same time. *There was that wink!* The audience was enthralled.

He also told of going to a movie or two with others, but he had never let any of it get serious. In fact, none of the dates went beyond friendship. George told the group that somewhere deep inside a still small voice was whispering *"Be protective of this one's feelings for she is not yours."* He continued explaining that he was told *"Don't lead her on. Don't give her any false expectations or illusions."*

So he obeyed and he was. Protective I mean. George began to tell the group how he knew--how he hoped that God would lead him to the one that was to be his one day and that was when he suddenly became speechless. He had just locked eyes with the enchanting red-headed and brilliant blue-eyed beauty he had seen at the gymnasium just weeks ago. What a time for the Lord to whisper *"That's her."*

As Mabel's eyes locked on to George's, electricity passed between them. Jennifer even shivered. It was profound. While hardly anyone else in the crowd seemed to notice, George and Mabel knew, they *knew*, they had found the one their souls had been searching for.

As George concluded his testimony, he realized that he was the one who had been on trial. He recognized that he was the one being issued an indictment, a life sentence. One without parole and one from which there would be no turning back. As he made his way back to Mabel, his heart was rejoicing. Somehow, he smiled to himself, this was a consequence he was happy to face. With a wink, he reached for her hand. With shimmering eyes, Mabel grasped his fingers in hers, feeling forever, feeling safe, feeling home.

Aunt Alice

As George grabbed a handful of quarters from the cute little wooden tray his nieces had made for him, Mabel was putting on her "eyes." She just couldn't go anywhere without her pretty blue peepers being made to stand out with just a touch of mascara. Soon she called out, "I'm ready, dear!" and George patted his pants pocket to make sure his wallet was there.

"I just know Aunt Alice will be so glad to see you, George. She's probably making the cornbread for you as we speak. My brownies are surely sitting on the counter cooling. She's such a love to make these for us. You know she hardly cooks anymore at all."

"I *do* know," George said with a sad sigh. He recollected times of old when he could walk into her house, the delightful aromas tickling his nostrils and making his belly growl. *Hmn. Maybe that's why I'm so thin now,* George thought to himself.

Almost as though reading his mind, Mabel said, "Aunt Alice sure could make a mean pot roast! I guess it's a good thing she can't cook as much these days since there's not much room in your tummy for extra."

Wryly smiling, George inhaled as much as he could while professing "I'm still as svelte as ever, Red. Plenty of room in here for more."

Snorting, Mabel poked him and watched his "flat" stomach resume its portly rotund shape.

As they drove through Asheville to the farm, each was preoccupied. Mabel was wondering how Alice would be doing--mentally--this time. She had just recently bought a new car and Mabel was hopeful that all of the fancy gadgets wouldn't be scary to Alice. The love was 84-years-old! It wasn't too long before Uncle Joe passed that she had given in to join the 21st century by investing in a smartphone.

Technology is tricky for us old-timers, Mabel pondered, *and for the really old old timers? It could be quite off-putting.*

George meanwhile was thinking about the farm and although it wasn't a huge place to keep up, for one lady it could be quite burdensome. With Alice's health deteriorating daily, he wondered how much longer she could live alone. He and his brothers did as much as they could, when they could, but still. This favorite aunt of his was going to soon need so much more.

"Do you think Jim and Jade will get enough pizzas or should we maybe stop and get some more? Or a bucket of chicken? I know Aunt Alice likes those spicy tenders we get. And the girls will surely need some of the Colonel's chocolate chip cookies!"

George started to respond but Mabel was still talking.

"Maybe we should get some extra coleslaw and biscuits too. Oh, wait: Alice usually makes cookies for the kids and with your cornbread, I'm sure there will be enough of that kind of stuff. But still…"

"Red. Slow down. Breathe."

He patted her leg, trying to soothe her. "You do this every time, honey. Calm down. Let someone else worry about the food for a change. Jade's no dummy. She knows what her kids like."

Reaching for the radio, George adjusted it until he found one of their favorite songs. Patting Mabel's leg a little more enthusiastically, he began singing his newest rendition of The Temptations' classic over her near protests. "Singing 'bout Mayyy-bell. May-bell!"

How could she love this man any more? She joined in with the finger-snapping portion of the song and the rest of the trip was pleasant. As they neared the Fletcher exit that would take them to the farm, Mabel murmured a silent prayer, asking God to one more time let this family gathering be filled with love, laughter, and lots of hugs and kisses from the kids.

Aunt Alice wouldn't be with them forever. And, even as aggravating as the ol' gal could sometimes be? No one ever doubted they weren't loved nor prayed over every day (and some of them twice a day!). Oh sure: her spit can was often mistaken for a drink by the younger babies but the ol' gal had to have one vice, right? Mild Dental Scotch Snuff, in its yellow can, was mentally added to Mabel's list.

"George, let's do make a stop at Ingle's. The least we can do is to get some candy for the kids. And maybe a bouquet of flowers for Alice. The pink ones. She really likes those. Since Uncle Joe isn't around to bring her fresh ones daily, maybe these will brighten up her window sill a smidge."

"Sounds good, Red. Why don't we also, 'just for fun,'" George made imaginary quotation marks in the air as he said this, "grab some tater wedges, some cheese bars, and some of those plastic balls for the girls to play with? I know that Crystal likes purple. I always seem to forget what color Amber likes: is it green or blue?"

Pausing for an instant, George continued. "Oh, and you know what, Mabes? We really should get some bubbles. Little Hopeful Opal will chase those things 'round and around as long as we keep blowing them."

George rarely spoke this much so Mabel gave him a curious look that he didn't see. Inwardly, she sighed as she thought about his anxiousness.

As they did their small amount of shopping at Ingle's, both were now feeling a little better about the trip. While Mabel swiped her Visa, George went over to the machines and, as usual, he inserted all of his quarters into those toy and gumball gadgets, just knowing some kid would have a happier day soon.

On their way again, George and Mabel held hands. They greatly anticipated seeing their sweet little nieces who really weren't so little after all but in their eyes, they'd always be their babies. As they drove up the long winding road to the farm, they could see Aunt Alice in her rocking chair on the porch surrounded by Jim, Jade, and the three girls: Crystal, Amber, and Opal. "My Family Jewels" was what Jim fondly called his gems. When they saw the yellow refurbished '67 Mustang come up the drive, both of the older girls came running while Opal stayed back. She was still a little shy. It never lasted long. One wookie from Uncle George and he'd soon have her wrapped around his finger.

As they pulled into the drive, Mabel's eyes misted over. She murmured a silent prayer of thanksgiving as she saw George's dear aunt, surrounded by so many of her loved ones. She couldn't help but feel a twinge of melancholy as she wondered if one day this would be her life and she'd be the one who was encompassed by nieces, nephews, and perhaps a sibling or two. Between her and George, there were a total of three extended families. The Good Lord had blessed all of their marriages with love and with mostly good health. The nine nieces and nephews were a tremendous extension of their legacies and Mabel happily sighed as she put those thoughts aside and purposed to make this time, this present with Aunt Alice, count more than ever. The losses of Big Jake, followed so closely by Grady and most recently Daisy, had hit them hard.

She pretended to not see George surreptitiously wipe his eye because she knew. She knew him inside and out and knew his thoughts were similar to hers. She lightly squeezed his hand, made a comment about it being pollen season, and hoped there were some brownies left. George raised her hand to his lips, placed a scratchy smooch on it, and winked at her. After all of these years, that wink still made Mabel giddy.

"Are you ready, Mrs. Harrison," George asked, as he put the Mustang in park.

Wiping one last bit of "pollen" from her own eyes, Mabel replied with a bright smile, "Why yes, Mr. Harrison. I do believe I am."

As Crystal and Amber scampered around them, and Opal peeped shyly from behind Aunt Alice's rocker, Mabel thought that Jim's family indeed were jewels and in the charm bracelet of life? Hers was twenty-four carat!

June 6, 2015

June 6, 2015. Twenty-five years since they first said their "I Dos" at the college's amphitheater, where they had been surrounded by friends and family.

We were just babies, Mabel thought. *Kids with stars in our eyes, dreams in our hearts, and love that was overflowing.* This time, however, they were sure, more sure than ever that what God had put together man would not pull asunder.

Still, Mabel was a little nervous.

"Valerie, are you sure everything is ready? I want it to be perfect! Did you get the sunflowers, the tables set? Is Aunt Alice really going to be here? Oh, and Mom? Oh, I do hope she doesn't say anything inappropriate. These days, one just never knows what will pop out of her mouth. Remember how her doctor warned us during this latter stage of her dementia that she might not even know us? What if she gets upset and starts wondering where she's at or--worse still--why she isn't the bride? Oh Val..."

Mabel's voice trailed off as tears threatened to mess up the mascara Lis had just applied, not an easy feat when one is nine-months pregnant and trying her best to reach Mabel's face over her extended belly. Melissa's belly not Mabel's. Hoping she wouldn't lose her balance, Lis reached for a nearby bottled-water, rubbing her tummy, and wishing this child would hurry up. Her due date had already passed and while on the one hand she wanted this unexpected fourth child to hurry and make his arrival, she also hoped he would wait until the ceremony was over.

While Jade and Melissa attended to their harried sister-in-love, Valerie made an overly-exaggerated pretense of double-checking that everything was correct. She chuckled to herself as she gave the slideshow she had prepared for this special occasion one last perusal on her iPad.

Oh Mabes, have I got a surprise for you!

With a self-satisfied smile, she reassured her sister that of course all was going as planned. She even took a moment to hold Mabes' hand, tell her how pretty she looked, and that yes, she was sure, this dress didn't make her hips look fat. *Ter.* Well, maybe she didn't say that last part out loud but she did think it for a fraction of a second.

Meanwhile, the twins were being corralled as Jim, Mark, and Will gave George some last-minute advice. "Just because you've done this once does not mean there isn't room for improvement," Mark told his big brother.

"Yeah, George. At this stage of the game you don't want to blow it. You know Mabel can still change her mind and find someone more...ahh...worthy? Richer? Suitable? Definitely a guy with more hair!" Jim ducked as Harry and Lloyd ran between his legs, nearly toppling him onto the couch in the changing room.

Not to be outdone, William added his two cents. Literally. He took two pennies from his pocket and offered them to George. With a questioning look, George waited for Will to explain.

"Well, when you married Mabel Lynn, you didn't have a dime to your name, George. What with inflation and such, I thought I'd start you two off with about the equivalent of that. Sort of like a dowry for my favorite brother-in-law. Don't spend it all at one time!"

The men all laughed and Shaun rolled his eyes as he checked himself in the mirror. *Old people,* he thought. *They sure have cra-cra ideas about what's funny.*

~~~~~~~~~~~~~~~~

After the ceremony, George and Mabel were basking from the well-wishes and the surprisingly sweet toasts from Jim and Mark. The deejay, with a little help from Shaun, began softly playing some romantic tunes on the stereo system. Taking her cue, Amanda dimmed the lights and Valerie regally approached the small podium that had been set up earlier for the vow renewal ceremony.

"Before the dancing begins, there's just one more portion of tonight's festivities to be shared. Most of us here have been witnesses to the love story of George and Mabel, right?"

Valerie waited as the crowd smiled and murmured in agreement with her. Ever the scene-stealer, she ingratiated herself once more, not quite bragging, but definitely insinuating herself as a large part of this memorable occasion.

"Please adjust your seats and feast your eyes on this video collection of moments shared between these two love birds. If a picture is truly worth a thousand words, then my work here is done."

Val brilliantly smiled and watched as the bride and groom--as well as the other guests--walked down Memory Lane, courtesy of all of the pictures she had taken since the photography bug had bitten her way back in 1978. The heartfelt song she had timed perfectly to conclude her presentation with and had been especially chosen for this slideshow by The Righteous Brothers--"Unchained Melody"--reached its climax. The crowd began to clap. George leaned in to kiss Mabel.

"Whoa ho; not so fast, Romeo," Valerie interjected.

Puzzled, Mabel looked at her sister, wondering what was going on. Nervously, she laughed, and before she could say another word, Val asked Miranda to queue the next song. Mindy giggled as she was momentarily cast into the spotlight and all eyes were on her. She twisted shyly in her purple sundress and tried to maintain her balance because it was her first-ever time wearing heels.

"There's one last picture I want to share with you. Actually, it's the one that got me started in the photography business. I happened upon it just a few weeks ago, as a matter of fact, while putting together this movie. Who knew--way back then-- that I would have gotten bitten by the picture bug while my sister Mabes was getting bitten by a bug of a different nature?"

Dramatic pause.

"The love bug!"

Oh great. What is that Valkyrie up to now, George wondered. Having been a brother all of his life, it was still hard for him to understand the complex relationship sisters shared.

Valerie gave Mindy the signal. She whispered to Shaun and he had the deejay start the music.

Mabel didn't know whether she should quietly excuse herself, pretend to go and check on Lulu Mom, or just be the sitting duck for what might happen next. She turned expectantly to her sister, who was mischievously smiling (never a good sign), and waited. Grasping George's hand in hers under the table, she clutched it tightly, and put on her best smile.

As the picture, an old Polaroid, came onto the big screen, George froze.

Was that...? Was that *the Little Red-Haired Girl? Impossible! And yet...yet... it all began to make sense. Red? His Red? The little girl he had saved from a near-drowning incident at Sliding Rock all those years ago? The shy girl who hadn't known how to properly thank him? The tousled-haired beauty who had given him his first kiss? That was Red? Mabel?!*

The melody to "Summer Nights" began to drift out as Valerie started her well-prepared speech. In the recesses of her mind, a distant memory was trying to catch Mabel's attention but it was lost as she listened to her darling sister's next words.

"Most of you know that Mabel has professed to *never* loving anyone but George. To *never* having courted anyone else, much less given a harmless smooch or two to some summer fling. But here, ladies and gentlemen, for your viewing pleasure, I have proof!"

Mabel's eyes were glued to the screen. There was not any doubt that that was indeed her in the tattered snapshot, even as old and grainy as it was. Oh yes: those gangly legs and frizzy red hair were undeniable. For further verification--as if any was needed--it was dated. *Sliding Rock, June 6, 1978.*

The memory flooded back to her. She had almost completely forgotten about it! After the kiss and her friends' ridicule, she had struggled to place that boy out of her mind and demanded her friends to do the same. Pinky swear even, and they had.

Brenda and Lisa Jo had long since placed this incident out of their minds as well, for that's what good friends do when they're ten-going-on-eleven. As they watched the slideshow, Mabel's childhood friends first stared in amazement, then reached across the table and locked little fingers with one hand and placed their other index fingers across their lips. Snickering at each other, they laughed as they recalled this moment from their youth.

Valerie continued with her spiel about the antics of kids and young love. The guests laughed and made remarks about what a cute little girl Mabel had been and wasn't that kiss just the sweetest thing? And then Valerie, high on her achievement of being the momentary center of attention with her spectacular reveal, uncharacteristically became speechless as she noticed the look on George's face. Her words faded as the notes fell out of her hand. She hadn't even gotten to the best part but...something was off.

Shaking her head in embarrassment at Val's antics, sheepishly Mabel turned to George. She was half-expecting him to be chuckling too at Valerie and her odd sense of humor as he usually did, but she was puzzled. What she saw in his eyes confounded her. Instead of shared laughter, there was wonder.

Questioningly, she looked at him. Bringing her hand to his lips, he placed a gentle kiss on her fingers and whispered, "Mabel. It was me."

"What?" Mabel asked. "What was you, George?"

She was quite confused by now.

"Red, it was *me*. That boy," he said, pointing to the overhead screen as she tremulously smiled at him with confusion in her tear-filled sapphire eyes, *"that boy was me."*

The song continued to play. George grabbed the nearby mic and began to sing softly to Mabel, changing the words as he so very often did.

"I saved your life when you nearly drowned"--and here he gave Mabel that infamous wink of his.

Ding ding ding! It all came together! Everything suddenly clicked. That summer of 1978 when Big Jake took them all to Transylvania County. The tall skinny boy at Sliding Rock. Why she had felt a sense of melancholy each time her Upward Bound groups went there on summer field trips. George was indeed her first kiss, her one, and her only.

Taking the mic from his hand, Mabel sang through her laughter and tears, asking him to tell her more.

As the two of them embraced, their guests joined them on the dance floor, not really understanding it all but, hey: George and Mabel had always had their own private way of communicating. Besides, who didn't enjoy dancing to the great songs of the seventies and eighties? They had come to witness their friends renew the vows they'd spoken to one another some twenty-five years ago and who could resist singing along with Danny and Sandy?

As the song reached its conclusion, Valerie was flustered. Picking up her notecards, she wondered: *What just happened here? And why are they laughing? What am I missing here?*

Her eyes darted to the happy couple, lost in each other, smiling dreamily, their love song still being sung. Hastily, with one hand on her hip and the other pointing into the air, she went over to them, demanding an explanation.

"What's going on here, Mabel Lynn? I've had that picture for...for...for a really long time. Back in the day, I was going to use it against you when you got on my nerves."

Pause.

Gulp.

"But, after that summer, something...changed between us and we started to be more than sisters. We started being friends," Valerie stammered. "I put the picture away in my hope chest and forgot all about it. I came across it a few months ago, and I just knew I had to include it for your slideshow--but not to embarrass you as much as to remind you that that summer, the summer of '78, changed my life."

"Oh Valerie Virginia." Affectionately Mabel pulled her sister in for a hug. "VV. You've been my best friend for as long as I can remember. How I love you!" Mabel kissed Val's forehead.

"Now sure, you used to get on my nerves, like those times when you'd follow me and my friends around. Constantly." Mabel flashed her sister her mean eyes. "And like when you'd sneak and listen to my calls from the kitchen phone. Or when you'd read my diary while I was helping Daddy in the tobacco field because you were 'too little' to help sucker tobacco."

Valerie smirked at this memory.

"But Val. This! This picture!" She pointed up at the image still frozen on the projector screen. Mabel's eyes filled with tears and she couldn't go on.

George interjected, putting his arm around his sister-in-love. "Valkyrie Revis, this time the joke is on you."
"Whatever do you mean, Possum?" Valerie only called George "Possum" when he got on her left nerve. Interrupting this tender moment with Mabes definitely classified as one of those times!

"I'm so glad you asked. For you see, that picture you took all those years ago? That boy your beautiful sister was kissing? Well, guess who he was?"

Incredulously, Valerie shook her head in disbelief.

"Unh-unh. For real? That was *you*, George? No way. *You* were my sister's first kiss?" She stared up at the Polaroid, searching for its truths.

Reaching for his bride, taking her into his arms, and leading her back to the dance floor, George replied over his shoulder, "Yes. And with God's blessing, I'll be her last."

With those words, the Harrisons glided away. Sheriff was singing "When I'm With You." Early in their relationship, the two had declared it as "their song" so it was only appropriate that it be played now as their recommitment to one another was taking place.

Val herself got chills as she re-examined with new eyes the Polaroid. The tall kid that her sister was tippy-toeing as far upwards as she could stretch before planting that smooch on him: *that was George?*

Oh my cow! Of course it was, she decided. *After all, isn't that what fairy-tales are made of?*

As the strands about the world standing still when the lovers were together lingered in the air and they engaged in another kiss, Valerie reached hurriedly for her camera, and captured this moment, this timeless moment of pure bliss while George and Mabel danced as though they were the only ones in the room.

Aha, Mabes. I've got you now. Oh, if we'd all only knew then what we know now.

Wiping the happy tears from her blinking eyes, she whispered a prayer of thanksgiving that she had been chosen for such a time as this. From the beginning, she was witness to one of the great love stories of her time and here she was now, still witnessing God working all things together for good.

Big Jake would be so proud.

George Jones Harrison

If you are scratching your head and wondering what's going on with my name, welcome to my world. Yes, I was named after both the legendary George Jones and one of those 1960's English band guys. Obviously, not Paul. Nor John. Ringo might have been a cool name but no, it was that other kid. Between my mother's love for the Beatles and Dad's love for country music, this firstborn son of theirs didn't stand a chance. In the womb, I didn't know whether to square dance or groove to rock and roll.

For a while, I was an only child. Dad was in the Army and during Vietnam, he was rarely home. When the conflict finally ended in 1975, I had gained a baby brother, James Alexander, and there was one more on the way: Mark Patrick. Thanks to the war, my brothers' names weren't as special as mine--although the music was still pretty groovy then. Some folks were doing what they called crossover music so between Willie Nelson, Glen Campbell, Crystal Gayle, and Anne Murray there was always something to tickle our ears with.

Of course, Momma had to have her soft rock. She'd often be found changing the radio dial whenever Johnny Cash would come on. She really didn't care for the man in black. Instead, she'd sing to Dad her version of "We Can Work It Out" but instead changed the lyrics to "You need to see it my way, Jake, lest you make a big mistake. Time will tell if I'm right or *you* are wrong." Yeah, she still had a thing for those Beatles. And I guess that's where I got my penchant for rewriting a few songs myself. *Thanks Mom!*

My early years were fun. The five of us lived in a small community called Mills River, located in western Henderson County, NC. I loved the outdoors and I often could be found traipsing through the woods on my way home from school. My brother Jim was young enough to think that I was cool and when I would get home, he'd follow me almost everywhere. I didn't mind. And although Mark wasn't quite as steady on his feet, he idolized his other brother Jim and wanted to be where he was. They had one of those love/hate relationships where they often couldn't stand to be in the same room yet within minutes would be found wrestling and playing some game that Jimmy seemed to always be making up.

As a child, I really enjoyed the cartoon *Peanuts.* I'd rush outside each Sunday morning to get our copy of the *Times-News* and dig out the comic section. I don't know what it was, but there was something about Charlie Brown's infatuation with the Little Red-Haired Girl that resonated with me.

As a young man, I seemed to be more drawn to auburn-haired ladies but...I don't know. I just never seemed to connect on the level to which most of the guys my age were. Oh sure, I dated. Went to the prom. But finding my lifelong companion--or even a summer fling--just wasn't something I was yearning for. For you see, my heart was already taken.

I'd been raised in a Christian home. Went to church often but not, pardon the pun, religiously. Near the end of my eighth-grade year, I accepted Jesus Christ as my Lord and Saviour.

It was one of those Sunday mornings that we had actually made it to church. I can't remember a word that the preacher said that day, but I *can* remember the conviction of sin that overwhelmed my young mind. Not conviction over any particular sin, just conviction that I was a sinner.

During the invitation to come to the altar, I can remember tightly grasping the pew in front of me. I remember thinking about being embarrassed to walk down the aisle. And I remember the relief I felt when I took that first step and didn't care anymore what people thought. I think that that first step was when the Lord quietly entered my life and taught me, through His Word, what was most important.

When I graduated from high school, I went on to college. It wasn't my plan. Truthfully, I didn't want to go but, by grabs, Grady and Daisy Harrison wanted their firstborn child to do what they had never had the opportunity to do. Mars Hill College seemed to be agreeable to us all and off I went.

I'd always loved history, especially World War II, so I worked towards getting my Bachelor's Degree in Social Sciences. Mabel and I met, married, and we made our home in Mars Hill. I went to work the summer after we graduated for a local electrical supply warehouse as a counter man and some 28 years or so later retired from CES as one of their purchasing agents.

So, my four years at Mars Hill culminated in a BS degree I didn't use but the woman I met there, my Mabel, my Red? Ahh, the history the two of us have made! Who knows? Maybe one day stories will be told of our adventures and our lives. All I can say is this simple man sure has a great life!

A Note From The Author

Hey there! I hope you enjoyed these stories about George and Mabel as much I enjoyed writing them. Ha! They practically penned themselves!

My plan is to bring you more sweet and funny tales of their adventures, their family, and their love. My notebook is already filled with ideas of their future escapades.

If you did like these, I invite you to follow George and Mabel on Facebook. Leave them a note. Share your love stories and your family's mishaps. Post photos of places you recognized throughout these pages. And by all means, go visit the places they have journeyed to.

Thanks for reading! There is much more to come!

Stefanie

https://www.facebook.com/workingtogetherforgood

Made in the USA
Columbia, SC
10 March 2020